Discovering the Pearl

A Journey to the Philippines

Kathleen Zayco Henschen

All Rights Reserved 2023
ISBN#9798864420799

Dedication

For my mother and father, Naty and Bong, now my angels, for nurturing my love for books and writing. For my sister, Gina, for sharing my love for writing. For my children, Evan, Erica, and Derek, and my husband Kent who give color and inspiration to my world.

In the heart of Asia where cultures unite,
Sits this island nation with resilience and might.

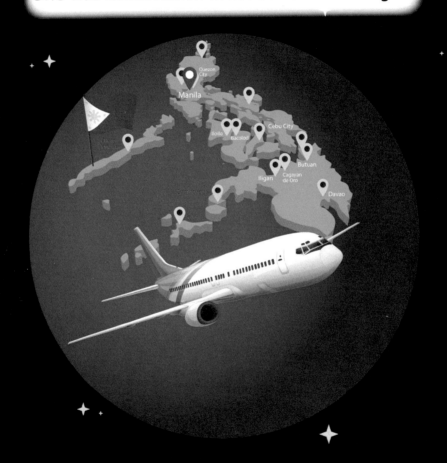

Known to many as Pearl of the Orient Seas.
For me, it's a place of love and laughter with family.

I put on my best clothes to visit my lola.
Together we explore the bustling capital Manila.

Mangoes, coconuts, purple ube so sweet,
I eat refreshing "Halo Halo", my favorite treat.

Volcanoes, lagoons and white sand twinkling beaches,
An underworld so beautiful teeming with corals and fishes.

Sea turtles, whale sharks, and tarsiers to admire,
It's a little piece of paradise anyone would desire.

Fields of sugar canes and rice paddies in the countryside,
Toiled by carabaos and farmers with smiles and pride.

From LUZON, VISAYAS, MINDANAO so wide,
The tapestry of colors it cannot hide.

So let's explore the Philippines you and me,
A land of wonder from sea to sea.

Though to other lands, I find myself roam.
The Philippine Islands I will always call home.

Common Words and Items in Tagalog

Mabuhay: A formal greeting. Its literal meaning is "long live" but used as a "Welcome"

Mano Po- A gesture when a young person puts the head to an elder's hand as a form of greeting and respect.

Lola/ Lolo: Grandmother/Grandfather

Halo- Halo- A refreshing desert made of shaved ice and ice cream topped with various fruits and sweets.

Ube- Purple Yam

Tarsier- An endangered small primate known for its big eyes. The Philippines is home to its sanctuary for protection.

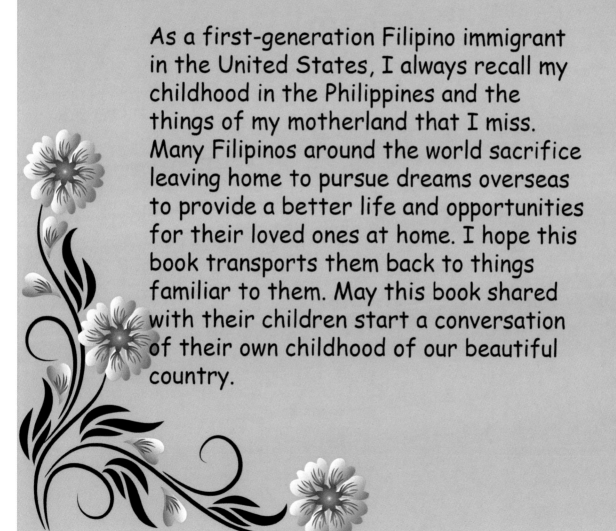

As a first-generation Filipino immigrant in the United States, I always recall my childhood in the Philippines and the things of my motherland that I miss. Many Filipinos around the world sacrifice leaving home to pursue dreams overseas to provide a better life and opportunities for their loved ones at home. I hope this book transports them back to things familiar to them. May this book shared with their children start a conversation of their own childhood of our beautiful country.

About the Author:

Mabuhay! My name is Kathleen Zayco Henschen. I am an English as a Second Language Teacher (ESL) for elementary students in a large and diverse public school district in Illinois. I am inspired daily by the resilience of the students from all around the world I have the awesome privilege of teaching. The richness of their backgrounds and cultures teach me about humanity. The stories of their memories of home inspired me to write this book of my own experience. Having moved to the US myself, I can often relate to the challenges they face. It is my passion to travel the world with my own children to let them know that each place is special. We live in a beautiful world! I am writing my first book of my birthplace the Philippines. I hope to continue to write about other countries I visit seen from the lenses of children.

Made in the USA
Monee, IL
14 December 2023

49198285R00017